www.mattshawpublications.co.uk

D1714539

With thanks to the following supporters of my work:

Steven Wexler, Gary Harper, Bernard Galpin, Amelia Sutherland, Karen Thomas, Jessica Shelly, Steve Chappo, James Herrington, Jean Kelly, Renee Luczynski, Cat Goy, Sharen Womack, Cipher66, Jennifer Brooks, Adam Searle, Mary Kiefel, Lucy Desbrow, Jill Rogers, Jacquetta B, Sophie Harris, Kristy Lytle, Melissa Potter, Jacqui Saunders, Nigel Parkin, Amber Chesterton, Billy Smith, Chris Peart, Jon Vangdal Aamaas, Peter Le Morvan, Gemma De-Lucchi, Julie Shaw, Marie Shaw, John Burley, George Daniel Lea, Donna Cleary, Lex Jones, Joanna Taylor, Karla Rice, Scott Tootle, Louise Turner, Kevin Doe, Andiboo, Sue Newhouse, Karen McMahon, Joy

Boysen, Mason Sabre, Anna Garcia-Centner, Angela McBride, Debbie Dale, Kelly Rickard Jennifer Eversole, Cece Romano, Jennifer Burg Palfrey, Michele Fleming, Jessica Richardson

A massive, massive thank you for supporting my work and being a part of my Patreon page!

Want your name listed here?
www.patreon.com/themattshaw

ROE V. WADE

MATT SHAW

A word from the author:

When this book was announced, I was accused of jumping on the bandwagon to earn money from a sensitive topic. Some people said I only wrote it in the hope of "boosting" my career. Neither comment is true.

For those who know me, you know I've been writing full-time for over ten years now (and writing for a lot longer than that). For those who don't know me, it would be a foolish move to release a book, on such a sensitive subject, in the hope of finding yourself an audience. After all, as social media comments have proven here, there are just as many people saying they'll never read my work again, as there are those who are praising me for writing this story. I am hoping the two will kind of equalise out and my career will carry on as it was but - honestly - my career doesn't matter. I am writing this book because the story came to me and I felt the *need* to write it.

Now some people have said that authors (and other creatives) should not get into politics but, pardon my French, that's bullshit. Creatives need to use their voice, in whatever way they can, to get their message out there. Otherwise, what is the point? Should songwriters not discuss current affairs in their music? Should films be purely fictitious, fantasy affairs with no basis in reality? No. We need to write, sing, film whatever is on our mind to help raise awareness and make people question what is happening around them. That being said, do I think my book will change the world? No. Of course it won't. If I can make one person think twice about what's going on in their country though, then my work here is done. In the meantime, for those who wish to ignore the "point", hopefully they'll just enjoy the fictitious story for, make no mistake, this is a work of fiction. I have taken the news from America (each state can now decide whether abortions should be legal or illegal) and I've gone past that to look at a much darker world where this current decision was just one step of many that were taken. First this right was removed, then another right, and another one, and another after that until we're left living in a world which suddenly feels a lot more claustrophobic than it had before. It's a horror story and one which will hopefully remain as nothing more than a story. That being said, it doesn't hurt if you read it as a "warning".

Now some people have been questioning my own beliefs and such and telling me I can still murder my baby because I am from the UK but, it's not about that for me and I've not really openly discussed where I fall within the great scheme of things. The whole point of this sorry affair is not whether abortion is right or wrong, it is - instead - the fact that it shouldn't be right for anyone else to decide what a person does to their own body. If you are Pro-Life then great, do not have an abortion. If you are Pro-Choice, live as you choose. What bothers me more than anything is that there is a loss of freedom by turning around and saying you cannot do such and such with your body. What bothers me more is when they follow it up by talking about the Bible and how it goes against their beliefs. Fine, fair enough. If your God is saying all life is sacred then go practise that in your life, or with people who also follow that religion. You cannot take your made-up rule from your made-up book and push it to other people, especially when they might not be Christians themselves. And that is before the argument that a foetus is just a group of cells. There is no capacity for thought, or consciousness, until the cerebral cortex is formed in the second trimester so... Until that point, it isn't life. Can it turn to life? Sure. But, at *that* point in time - it's not there yet. Give people back their right to decide what to do with their own body and how to live their life and you, in turn, can go and live your life as you choose.

The biggest piece of shit I've read since all this came to light is from some twat in Texas. I forget his surname sadly, as I blocked him pretty fast, but... Austin turned around to me and said, 'I'm glad it was overruled because it goes against my beliefs.' That's it. That was his argument, as he continued talking about God to someone who, quite frankly, doesn't give a shit about God.

Want to hear something funny to end this mild-rant? I released a book mocking the Bible and these same good Christian folk didn't bat a fucking eyelid. But what a woman does with her body? Holy shit can they kick up a stink. The good news is that these same fuckers who are demanding women lose the right over their bodies will probably never get to see a naked woman, without first visiting a morgue and paying the mortician a hefty fee. Even then the corpse will probably give them the cold shoulder.

Yeah. I went there. Sorry.

ROE V. WADE

HISTORY

In **1969** Norma McCorvey became pregnant with her third child. She wanted an abortion but, under Texas law, she wasn't permitted to have one as abortions were illegal, unless they were necessary to save the mother's life.

Seeking legal help, and under the legal pseudonym *Roe*, Sarah Weddington and Linda Coffee filed a lawsuit on Norma's behalf. The lawsuit was filed in the U.S Federal Court against Norma's local district attorney, Henry Wade. The suit alleged that Texas's abortion laws were unconstitutional. A three-judge panel of the U.S. District Court for the Northern District of Texas ruled in her favour and declared the relevant Texas abortion statutes were unconstitutional. This ruling was appealed to the Supreme Court of the United States.

On January 22, **1973**, the Supreme Court issued a 7-2 decision holding that the Due Process Clause of the Fourteenth Amendment to the United States Constitution provided a fundamental "right to privacy", which protected a pregnant woman's right to have an abortion. It was this decision which struck down many federal and state abortion laws. It also fuelled an ongoing abortion debate in the United States about whether abortion should be legal, to what extent, who should decide the legality of it and - what the role of moral and religious views in the political sphere should be.

The Supreme Court's decision in the case of Roe V. Wade was the most controversial in U.S. history.

In June of **2022**, The Supreme Court - in a 5-4 decision - overturned Roe V. Wade. As a result, almost half the states are expected to outlaw, or severely restrict, abortion. The new laws, related to a highly restrictive new Mississippi abortion law, will affect tens of millions of people around the country, with many having to cross state lines to seek reproductive health care.

The year is 2032.

All states have outlawed abortion due to
increasing pressures from within the
respective government parties.

1

TODAY

Heavily medicated so as to cause less stress to the baby she didn't want, Cate Hart watched the brown sludge filter down the feeding tube, up to where the tubing disappeared under her skin and into her stomach. Even through the med-induced fog, she wished nothing more than to grab the tube and rip it from her body. The desire to eat and drink nothing, to slowly wither and fade away than to endure any more of *this*.

Stripped naked, in a room where the temperature was carefully monitored so as to not hurt the unborn children, Cate was just one of many women. They were all secured to the padded wall, held in place by uncomfortable metal bars; a bar around their neck, the top of each arm, their wrists, the top of their thighs and their ankles. Even if the women weren't all pumped full of drugs to keep them half-sedated, there was no wriggle room, or chance of escape. They were there for the duration, held in place with their legs apart and "cups" attached to both anus and vagina; ready to collect any waste not caught by the drainage tubes pushed through to both bowel and bladder.

For the most part, the women were silent. On rare occasion, a quiet sob would break through the medicated state of mind but, it was always promptly silenced by a worker giving a quick burst of gas through the clear mask over the women's faces. One quick gulp of "toxic" air and, their bodies would go limp once more and their minds would be fogged again.

The room itself wasn't silent. Machines clicked, clunked and beeped away, almost in unison with one another. The "toilet tubes" (a phrase coined by one of the workers there) would also make noise as they sucked out any waste, from within the women, the moment their sensors picked it up. Then, of course, there were the workers. Masked men whose job it was to monitor the various pieces of equipment, and insure that both mother and child were kept alive and well.

For the women trapped there, the days were the same. Workers would come and go. They'd check on the machines, they'd note down the vitals and they'd leave again -

never once trying to engage in conversation with the "patients".

They weren't patients. From the moment the women were pulled to the facility, and dragged kicking and screaming down to Room 101, they were nothing more than pieces of meat. As they were strapped to their place on the wall, some even asked *what about their rights*? The question was always left unanswered but, only because everyone knew the answer. The women had no rights anymore. Not after they found themselves with an unwanted pregnancy. The tragic thing was, even had they been happy about being pregnant and done all they could to keep the baby and welcome it to the world, they still had less rights than their male counterparts.

This was the world now. Instead of progressing, it had taken massive backward steps and, it was only getting worse.

2

Time of day: Unknown.

The automatic doors opened, and a woman's cries bellowed into the room as she was pushed in, strapped to a trolley.

One of the workers turned to see the new addition to the room and immediately put his hands up and said, 'Whoa, whoa, whoa… Wrong room.'

'Other one is full.'

'I don't care, she ain't coming in here…'

Through the conversation the Black woman was screaming that she'd only had a moment of madness. Temporary insanity. She wanted the baby. She did. She'd do anything she could to look after it and raise it to be a valued member of society. Her pleas were ignored as the worker continued to argue with the delivery team.

'You know the drill... Get the fucking Negro out of here.'

'Jesus fucking Christ, does it really matter the skin colour when they're still going to spit out another recruit?!'

'Not my rules. Get that bitch gone and - if anyone asks - I'll just say you got lost.'

'The room's fucking full, man...'

'Then you know what to do. Again, not my rules.'

The woman's screams increased in volume as they wheeled her trolley back out of the room and into the far-reaching corridor beyond. The automatic doors closed behind the worker as he shook his head and went back to his tasks at hand.

'Fucking newbies,' he muttered through the mask, unaware that the woman's passionate cries had pulled Cate a little further from her brain-fog. Her mind immediately played back what had brought her to this room and - unseen by the worker, for now at least - a single tear rolled down her cheek.

3

BEFORE

Christmas morning.

Jack was pulled from his deep dream by the sound of his wife, Cate, crying from the ensuite bathroom. It wasn't the start to his Christmas which he had been expecting, especially given how they'd both gone to bed in high spirits.

Confused, he tossed the covers back and climbed from the warmth of his bed before making his way across the carpeted floor to where she'd closed the door separating bathroom and bedroom. With a gentle knuckle, he quietly knocked on the door.

'Cate? You okay?'

She didn't answer. Instead, he heard as she tried to stifle the tears.

'Cate?'

'Be right out,' she said, the moment she was able to whilst sounding as "normal" as possible.

'You crying?'

'I'm fine.'

'What is it?'

She didn't answer.

'Cate, can you open the door?'

From the other side, Cate pulled back the bolt. Jack turned the handle and pushed the door open to reveal his wife, sitting on the toilet with her panties still around her ankles. Her eyes were red-raw from crying. Before Jack needed to ask what was wrong, he noticed the pregnancy test sitting on the side, next to the sink. He felt his heart sink. Now the first question to mind wasn't to ask what was wrong, but to ask *how*. Since contraception had been banned, he'd got a vasectomy. The whole point of that was to stop this from being able to happen. The question of "How" turned to "Is it mine" in his head; both questions he managed to refrain from asking.

'I'm sorry,' Cate said.

Jack couldn't help but wonder *why* she was sorry. Was she sorry because she had been cheating on him and now it had come back to bite her on the arse? Or, was she sorry that she was pregnant? Maybe the apology was for both?

Jack just stood there, unsure what to say or do. After what felt like an eternity to both, he forced a smile and said, 'Merry Christmas.'

4

Cate was sitting at one end of the breakfast table with Jack sitting on the other. Their young son, Hunter, was sitting between them. As was tradition on Christmas morning, Cate had cooked bacon, hash browns, over-easy-eggs and link sausages. It wasn't the only morning she cooked such a breakfast but, sometimes she threw together something far simpler. With how little she and Jack were eating, she wished she'd stuck with the "simpler" option today.

At least Hunter seemed to be enjoying his. Watching him eat, she was unsure whether he'd even stopped to take a breath since his first mouthful. But then, he was probably eating fast so as to get to the presents which were waiting in the next room. A rule of the house: No presents until after breakfast. Clearly he was keen to see what was waiting for him beneath the Christmas tree.

Just as Cate and Jack hadn't really eaten anything, neither had they spoken much either. Not to one another anyway. They'd both wished Hunter a happy Christmas and asked if Santa had been to see him; every year they left a few parcels at the end of his bed and said they were from Santa Claus.

Cate glanced from her son up to her husband. He was staring down at his breakfast, toying with it with his fork in pretty much the same way she'd been doing. He had a concerned look on his face. She couldn't blame him given what she was feeling too. Pregnant? The first had nearly killed her and they'd both talked - soon after - stating they wouldn't go through it again, just in case. That and the fact they couldn't really afford a second child. Yet, here they were… She was pregnant again.

Out of the blue, seemingly unable to hold the question in anymore, Jack asked, 'Is it mine?'

Cate froze with her mouth slightly agape. A part of her wondering whether she'd heard him properly, or - at the very least - understood.

'Is it yours?' she asked, to clarify his question.

He nodded.

Hunter looked up and asked, 'Is what yours?'

Thinking quickly on her feet, Cate answered, 'The big present under the tree. Your daddy wants to know if it is his.' She turned back to Jack. With the look on his face, he hadn't even heard his son. If he had then he was ignoring him. Cate said, 'Of course it's yours! Who's else would it be?'

Jack shrugged.

Cate said again, 'It's yours!' Knowing there was clearly stuff the "adults" had to talk about, she turned back to Hunter. 'If you're done, why don't you go and pick yourself a present from under the tree. Daddy and I will be in to watch you open it in a minute.'

Hunter didn't need to hear the offer twice. Since November he had been excited about Christmas and - now it was here - he just wanted to rip open all of the presents. He jumped up from the table and headed out of the dining room and towards the living room.

Jack and Cate sat in silence for a moment.

'It's yours,' she said again. 'I can't even believe you asked me that.'

'I had a vasectomy.'

'I wasn't sure… I thought I was just late. It happens sometimes. Especially when I'm stressed… But when the period didn't come, I went online…'

'… The point of the snip is to…'

Cate continued, 'They're not 100% effective. They can fail.'

Jack didn't even bother to finish what he was saying. He just sat there, shocked. Of all the ways for his Christmas to play out, this was not something he'd ever considered.

Cate continued, 'It's rare but it can happen.' She paused a moment and said again, 'I'm pregnant.' She let the words sink in for a moment. Then, she asked, 'So what now?'

After a moment's thought, Jack answered, 'Now, we start practising our smiles.' He paused a moment and then, with some effort, forced his mouth to smile.

Cate burst into tears.

5

The whole of the country had gone crazy. To begin with, it was just a few states which chose to make abortions illegal. Those seeking one, if living in such a state, were forced to travel elsewhere if they wanted to terminate their pregnancy. However, when more and more women started travelling to other states to get rid of their unwanted child, pressure was mounted on those states who still chose to give the woman the right to have a choice. They want to support such people? Fine. Then, by law, they must pay a heavy - almost state-crippling - tax. They managed to pay such a tax then, fine, the clinics which offered the procedures suddenly needed an extremely expensive, and hard to come by, licence in order to remain open. They managed that too, then - okay... The state senator often came to a violent end at the hand of "extremists".

Now there was never any proof that these murderers were hired but, it was certainly no coincidence that the next senator to step into the role was "Pro-Life". As soon as they were in office, abortions were made illegal. The senator "won" the people over by using the "saved money" to make other changes to the state, which the people *did* approve of.

Distract them with something good, and do something bad; a trick which politicians all over the world had mastered.

Fast forward to today and there were special task forces set up to keep an eye on pregnant women. If a woman purchased a testing-kit then their name was put on a register, along with their address details. If they gave false details then it was considered a serious crime given it showed ill-intention to the unborn child. Once caught, they were usually imprisoned for the term of their pregnancy. If they gave their real details then - randomly - they were followed by members of the task force. If they got on with their lives, happy to be expecting then they'd never know they had an extra shadow. The presence of the task force was only ever felt if they tried to do anything stupid, which might bring the pregnancy to a premature end. In those instances, no one really knew *exactly* what happened. They just knew that the woman was taken off to a special facility to help with the duration of their pregnancy. Not that they ever came back.

Instead, after the nine months were up, the rest of the family suddenly disappeared too. Word would be left that they'd be given a new home - someplace else - as a "congratulations on a difficult pregnancy" from the government. No one questioned why these people never got back in touch with their friends because, rumour had it, if you asked too many questions then - you too would get a late-night visit before disappearing. Whether that was the truth or not, no one really knew. At the same time, no one really wanted to take the risk.

Today, even if hormones were giving them hell, it was rare to see an unhappy, or emotionally unstable pregnant woman. Instead, they all went around with smiles on their faces with most also boasting about how happy they were to be expecting…

But not everyone could keep the smiles up and *Roe V. Wade* was just the first of many rulings to be overturned.

6

TODAY

The trolley's wheels squeaked as they trundled down the sterile corridor of white walls, white floor and white ceiling. The worker who'd just been turned away from Room 101 was still bitching about how they wouldn't make room for this patient. Yes, she was Black and, yes, there were rules in which Black and white folk were kept separate these days but - to him - he never saw "colour", he saw "people". But then, he didn't agree with any of this. Not that he said anything. He didn't have to agree with it. For him, Claude, it was a job. A means to an end; a way to pay the bills and keep the roof over his head.

As the poor woman continued screaming for her release, Claude pushed her past Room 102; the room reserved for the Blacks.

Room 102 was at capacity at the moment. Unlike Room 101, which had other areas set aside for pregnant women, there was only one room for the Black women and, when that was full...

The automatic doors to Room 103 opened and Claude pushed the trolley in. He was greeted by another of the site's long-term workers; a weird, bearded cunt who made most people feel uncomfortable given his *love* of the job.

He stopped the trolley from being pushed deeper into the room and said, 'Hold up! This one's been done already, hasn't it?'

Claude was getting sick and tired of people stopping him from doing his job. This was his last drop-off for the day before he'd get to clock out and head home. All he wanted to do was take the person to where they needed to be and then leave. 'What are you talking about?'

'The skin! Black as soot! This fucker's clearly been crisped already.' He laughed at his own "joke", exposing his grimly yellow teeth and blatant racist attitudes.

Claude didn't laugh. Instead, he shook his head in disgust - not that he said anything. He hated the attitude of people like this. Fine, all of this was law now and there was nothing someone like him could do about it, but - that didn't mean those upholding the law had to be dicks about it. But then, why was he surprised? Rewind to a time before all of this, when Blacks were allowed to mix with whites, when people could use contraception, choose to have an abortion, could marry whoever in the fuck they wanted to marry... Even back then, there were still *some* people in positions of authority who took things too far. Growing up, he'd lost count the number of times he'd read about a Black person being gunned down by white officers, despite appearing to be complying with all that was being asked of them. Or how many times white folks turned on each other just for having differing political views. The days of living *your* life were gone long before any of the changes brought about by Roe V. Wade. Until working here though, Claude never realised just how fucking shitty things really were.

'I'll take it from here,' the racist piece of shit said as the woman screamed for her life.

'I don't understand why we do this,' Claude said, uncharacteristically. His words, so out of the blue, stopped the worker in his tracks as he started to pull the trolley away.

'Why we do this? Because we don't need more of their kind running around, do we? All about keeping the numbers controllable,' was the answer.

Claude watched as he wheeled the trolley towards the incinerator in the far corner of the room. The woman's screams increased in pitch.

7

Claude climbed into the front of his 4x4. He put his head in his hands for a moment and took in a deep intake of unsteady breath. Slowly, he released it. He lifted his heavy head from his hands and wiped his eyes dry. All things considered, he thought he'd done quite well to get out of there without crying. Admittedly it wasn't a crime to show emotions, not yet anyway, but - even so... He wouldn't have won the trust of his fellow colleagues had they seen him crying over a drop-off; especially a Black one.

He glanced back at the facility. A plume of black smoke billowed from one of the chimneys. Knowing what it was, his heart felt heavy to the point of being almost painful. Not wanting to see it anymore, he started the vehicle up and spun it around in the near empty parking lot so that the facility was behind him. In front of him, there was the parking lot's exit point and the long road home. All he had to do was carry on driving and yet...

He looked back at the facility via the rear-view mirror. His eyes drawn to the smoke.

At least the woman wasn't screaming anymore, he thought.

A tear dribbled from his eye. He quickly wiped it away. There was no point in crying for her, it didn't change anything, and it certainly didn't make anything better. Also, the last thing he needed was to go home with a face flushed from crying. His wife, Lauren, had warned him about taking this job but, what was he supposed to do? They needed the money and, it was the first job offered. She'd always said he was "too sensitive" for this kind of work. He didn't need to prove her right.

He took his eyes from the rear-view mirror and pulled his phone from his jacket pocket. Quickly he tapped a message out, *On my way*, and - he sent it to Lauren. All being good, she'd start preparing dinner, so it was waiting for him when he got in. He just hoped it wasn't barbecue.

8

Usually when Claude left "the office", he was able to leave "work" there. Home was home, work was work. Today had been the first time he'd had to take someone down to the run-off room though and, it was playing on his mind. Whenever he closed his eyes he could see the fear in the poor woman's face as he wheeled her down the corridor. He could hear her screams and her pleas to be released. Then, he could see that asshole's face and the look he had after his supposed joke. He was used to the nastier side of society now but, this job was really highlighting it for him. What made it worse,

if "worse" could be such a thing, was that -
he knew today wasn't going to be a one-off.
He knew he would be taking more people
there, he knew more helpless and terrified
individuals would be taken to the
incinerators. He was doing his job but, in
the eyes of God - was he a murderer having
led the people to the rooms in which they
died?

'You're quiet today,' Lauren said as they
sat down to the meatloaf she'd prepared for
their dinner.

Claude smiled. 'Busy day. Just tired.'

He took a sip from his chilled wine.

'Anything you want to talk about?'

His smile broadened and he said, 'I'm
good.'

'One day you'll tell me.'

It wasn't that Claude didn't want to talk
to her about his day. He would have loved to

have been able to vent to someone about it, as opposed to carry all the weight on his tired shoulders. He couldn't though, because of the non-disclosure agreement they'd made him sign. He was fine to say where he worked, but he couldn't say *what* happened within the facility's walls. Instead, they each had a script they could recite, if anyone asked; nothing special, just a vague tale of make-believe which would give the "normal" people hope. After all, the truth would have most likely led to more riots and, over the years, the government had seen enough of those.

Claude and Lauren were in their late twenties. A young couple, they had been together for a couple of years now. Lauren worked hard in an office downtown, mostly doing admin work for her bosses - which, of course, included the fetching of their coffee. Claude, meanwhile, had studied as a marine biologist but when no work was available in that field - he took what he could get just so as to keep the rent payments up.

Outside of work, Claude was happy. So was Lauren. They were childhood sweethearts, having gone to the same school and college. The only time they were apart was when she left college to work in the office, and he continued his studies in further education. Even then, they weren't "apart" in that they stopped seeing each other. She just went to work whilst he went for further schooling.

As with most couples, they had a plan which had kind of been derailed thanks to how hard it was to do more than "get by" in life. Even the white wedding Lauren had dreamed of, this big fairytale fantasy, had been swapped for a quick ceremony in a civil hall thanks to the ever-rising cost of living expenses. Still, the way she saw it, she'd sooner be married to the man she loved than stay engaged for life because they couldn't afford the thousands it would have costed for her ideal ceremony.

Marriage was one thing, owning a house was another - something they were saving for as best as they could be, as it was, their combined monthly wages didn't leave much in the way of savings. Then, of course, like many young couples around them - there was the desire to start a family of their own...

Lauren said, 'Okay let's start with something simple.'

'Something simple?'

'Yes. About work.'

'You know I can't.'

Lauren giggled. 'I'm your wife. I won't tell.' Before Claude could protest again, she asked, 'What are they like?'

'They?'

'The rooms. Are they nice? Is it all luxurious.'

Claude couldn't help but to laugh. As part of the script they gave people, they implied it was like a plush hotel where the ladies would be pampered throughout their pregnancy. A far cry from the truth.

Lauren continued, 'Is it nicer than where we live, for example?'

'I can't...'

Before Claude could finish his sentence, Lauren cut him off, 'Because I'm pregnant.' She giggled again; this time mostly driven by nerves. 'I was thinking that, if it is nicer there... We could lie and say we don't want it so; you know, I could have a few months of luxurious living for a while…'

Claude said nothing. He just sat there, stony-faced.

Slowly, Lauren's smile faded.

9

Lauren watched Claude as he continued eating his mashed potato. She was waiting for him to say something or, at the very least, show some emotion but - he gave away nothing. The longer the silence continued, the most she wondered whether he was even happy with the news. In her head, there'd been an entirely different reaction.

'Are you going to say something?' she asked when she could take the silence no more.

Claude stopped chewing for a moment. It was clear from his expression that he was thinking of the "right" thing to say. When he thought he had it, he swallowed his mouthful. 'Don't say you don't want the baby.'

'Jesus, I was joking.'

'Even so, don't even joke about it.'

'You know I want it! Admittedly I wasn't planning on getting pregnant so soon after you started your new job but, even so... I'm happy! It was just a stupid comment in case I was missing out on something really nice, you know? From how it sounds, these women who don't want their baby are being given a life of luxury whilst we go from pay-check to pay-check so, I was just saying...'

'I know what you were saying and - don't.'

'Okay!' Lauren didn't understand why Claude was reacting like this. She found the whole thing to be ridiculous but, even so, she said, 'I'm sorry.'

Silence descended between the two of them once more as he resumed eating.

'Are you happy at least?' she asked. 'I thought we both wanted this.'

It wasn't that Claude didn't want a baby, it was just - it had been a long, ugly day. His mind was torn apart from all he'd seen today, not helped by the fact he believed he could still smell the smoke from back at the facility. He was having a hard time putting all the horror to the back of his mind, to make room for the news which - on any other day - would have been good. Even so, he realised he was being an asshole.

'I'm sorry,' he said. 'I'm just tired and stressed…'

'Stressed? Because I'm pr-...'

'From work. It's been a long day. To answer your question, yes... Yes, I'm happy.' He forced a smile.

Even though Lauren knew it had been put-on for her benefit, she smiled back. Claude got up from his chair and walked around to where she was sitting. He leaned down and kissed her on the forehead.

'I'm happy,' he said again.

When he stood up straight, Lauren stood too and cuddled into him. Snuggling against him, she could feel that he was tense. For someone so "happy", he was having a funny way of showing it. Despite feeling that all wasn't okay, Lauren didn't say anything. She just hoped that he was in shock and that, once it had sunk in, he'd be happier and more relaxed with it. She blamed herself for his reaction. She should have waited and given him more time to decompress from the day as opposed to blurting it out over dinner. She guessed it could have come across as an ambush.

In the hope of making a weird atmosphere more bearable, Lauren said, 'I love you.'

There was a slight delay before, 'I love you too.'

Lauren felt Claude's grip tighten around her but, the way he said it... Everything just felt as though it were unnatural. Worse, it felt forced. She didn't question him.

10

Time: A little after one in the morning.

Claude was lying in bed. On his back, with his hands tucked under his head and elbows jutting out to the side, he was staring up at the ceiling. Whilst tired when he went to bed, the moment he laid down - his brain kicked into overdrive with thoughts of their future going round and round in his beaten mind.

The biggest thing on his mind was how much he hated his job. In such a short space of time, he'd seen things which would bring bigger people to their knees, and he couldn't help but wonder what else the facility hid behind its thick, concrete walls. The problem was, with a baby on the way, he knew he was stuck in his current role. It had been hard enough getting that job and, they needed every penny they could get. He couldn't just leave and claim benefits. Fair enough, he might have been able to before but... Not with a kid on the way...

What made it harder was that he felt like he was truly alone too. He had Lauren but the NDA he signed basically cut her from that part of his life. If anything was bothering him at work, he had two choices: Swallow it down, or discuss it with management. From what he had seen so far, he knew management wouldn't give a flying fuck about it. Worse than that, with what he had seen there so far, he imagined they'd have no problems in making him disappear if he did speak up and say anything about what was going on there. After all, why let someone rock the boat when they can just as easily throw them off the boat. And, to stop them from speaking out, how easy it would be to hold them under the water until they were permanently quiet.

To think, when he first got the job, they went out and celebrated with the best of champagne. Finally, they thought, things were starting to fall into place and yet now - lying there in the dark - Claude couldn't help but feel as though his perfect future was even further away than before. The only thing he couldn't understand was - why? He'd studied and worked hard his whole life. How come he was getting punished like this? Or, was this what everyone went through and - like him - they too suffered in silence? Was this living now? And this was the world he was going to bring a baby into? The world was broken. Why would anyone want to bring another life into this shit-show?

'Can't sleep?'

Lauren's voice shattered his thoughts - and probably at the best possible time as, Claude knew his musings were heading into dangerous territory.

'No,' he said.

'Me neither.'

Lauren rolled over and snuggled into him. Claude left one hand tucked behind his head. With his other arm, he reached around Lauren and pulled her closer.

As they lay there, in the quiet of night, he lied to himself, *Maybe tomorrow will be better?*

11

BEFORE

'Oh you must be so thrilled!'

Cate laughed. 'One word for it.'

'Was it planned?'

Cate couldn't help but think it was a bit of a weird question. In a country where abortions were illegal, punishment with a long-term prison sentence, and contraception was also against the law; only an idiot would choose to have intercourse in the old-fashioned way. Now, those who wished to avoid parenthood stuck to alternative ways to pleasure one another;

oral, anal, toys, etc, or - like Jack - the man would get the "snip". That being said, Cate guessed there must have been some stupid people out there who tried the old "pull out" method, not thinking that they'd get pregnant in such a fashion. *Jesus, the thought of those people becoming parents...*

'Well, it wasn't planned. Actually, Jack had a vasectomy not long after our last child but,' Cate hesitated a moment as she chose her next words carefully, 'I guess God had a plan.'

'Amen. God does indeed have a plan.'

Cate swallowed the bile down. She hated this new wave of Christianity which had taken over the country. People picking and choosing parts of the Bible to believe in and which parts to entirely ignore because it didn't serve their life. Or rather, she hated the way these people *forced* others to live that lifestyle too. For Cate, it should have all been about choice. If someone chose to follow God, okay. If someone chose to follow another path then, that too was fine. What wasn't fine was dictating how other people should live and yet - here they were.

And of course, the Bible is all against abortion stating that all life should be protected. Never mind whether it could cause the death of someone else, be it through medical means or mental health. Only last week, a rape victim promptly killed herself after being forced to give birth to her rapist's child. Try talking to Christians about that scenario? *Well God has a plan.* Or, more insultingly, *God works in mysterious ways.* As Cate's work colleague continued praising the Lord, Cate couldn't help but to think, *Fuck your God.*

'Also,' her colleague continued, 'it would be nice for little Hunter to have a brother or sister, don't you think?'

'It most certainly would,' Cate said as her mind started questioning why - on that fateful Christmas Day - they hadn't just taken a fucking coat-hanger and scraped out her insides. Keeping up the pretence of "being happy", she continued, 'I'm sure he'd love a brother!'

'I'll say a prayer that's what he gets then.'

Cate smiled. 'Thank you.'

Inside her head, she was contemplating murdering her colleague. She'd never actually do it but, sometimes it was nice to give in to the bad thoughts and let them mentally play out in her mind as a way of stress relief. She'd often found herself hoping that the country never got the technology to read people's minds. If they did, she'd surely be locked up for life.

'Well,' Cate said, 'that's my break over… Best get back to work.' She pushed herself away from the small table in the office cafeteria and started to collect her belongings, ready to take back to her desk space in the open plan office.

'Wait a minute,' her colleague said suddenly.

Cate froze.

Her colleague continued, 'You've not finished your shake yet?'

'I was going to take it with me,' Cate lied.

Once found to be pregnant, all women received a supply of shakes which contained a number of supplements deemed healthy for the baby. A brown, sludge-like mixture - it was rancid to taste and there was no scientific proof it helped those who actually drank it. But for the baby? Apparently it was the best source of nutrients. Cate called bullshit long ago. She just had it pegged as another way of keeping control of people. Especially after the government put in a "reward" for those who reported any non-drinkers.

'I was going to finish it at my desk,' Cate lied.

'Are you not supposed to drink it within a certain time?'

'Oh yes. Of course. Silly of me. I'd forget my head if it weren't attached.' She picked the half-full drink up and downed the thick remnants. When she swallowed, she tried to hide the involuntarily shudder.

She'd thought she had done a good job until her colleague said, 'It's vile, isn't it?'

Another lie, Cate said, 'It's not that bad.' She smiled and, with that, she threw the empty bottle in the trash and left the room. Aware that her colleague could still see her through the large pane of glass separating the breakroom from the corridor (another way to keep an eye on people, no doubt), Cate continued to smile right the way back to her desk.

12

Cate couldn't wait for maternity leave to come about, if only for the fact it meant she could stay home and not have to sit hour in, and hour out, forcing a smile to stay plastered on her face. At the moment, whenever she went home, she did so with an aching jaw. Her husband, Jack, must have experienced the same as - once home - neither of them seemed to smile. At least, not when the curtains were closed, and the outside world was shut out from their lives. Cate was just grateful her company gave a decent maternity package.

The smile wasn't only for the benefit of her colleagues, and anyone else who may have been watching. A part of her brain hoped that she might be able to fool herself too. The more she smiled, the more happiness she would feel towards the baby growing inside her? It didn't work. With each passing day, she found herself resenting it more and more and - in her mind - she'd often play out various scenarios in which she could "accidentally" kill it. She could fall down the stairs at work, blaming someone for shoving her? Although, pregnant women were supposed to use elevators wherever possible so - if she went that route, she would have to explain why she was near such a flight of stairs in the first place. She could eat the wrong food? Go to a restaurant and purposefully cross-contaminate her own meal with a mixture that could kill the child? But then, pregnant women weren't supposed to be eating out. Instead, they were meant to stick to their special shakes. Even if she could get permission to eat out, she'd then have a battle to prove it was the restaurant which poisoned her. And if she won? She'd automatically make it harder for other women to go out and enjoy meals on special occasions. After all, the governments would surely clamp down on such activities if there were increased risks to the unborn.

Sometimes Cate would sit at her work desk and wonder whether there could be a way to skip the country. Fly somewhere else - anywhere else - and start a new life somehow but, again, it wasn't possible. Even if they had the money in their savings account to afford it, pregnant women weren't allowed to travel internationally for fear of exposing the baby to radiation; never mind the fact that the dose received on planes is miniscule. Even so… If they were to skip the country, they needed to do it before she'd taken a pregnancy test. Once that kit was purchased… The government had all her details and that was that. Her freedom was severely restricted.

As Cate's days passed slowly by, she grew ever increasingly frustrated that the unborn child - without the ability of thought - had more rights than she seemed to have at *any* stage of her own life. What made the frustration worse was, there was nowhere she could vent such thoughts. At least, not anywhere other than home, behind locked doors and, that wouldn't have been fair on Jack. There was no point ranting about it to him when he was feeling the same. Working longer hours, in order to get the finances to support the child after it was born, Jack's life had changed too, just in different ways.

In the hope of escaping her own crushing thoughts, Cate turned to the large windows which overlooked the city. Out there, from this height, the city looked beautiful, and, for a moment, you could almost fool yourself into thinking that it was. From this height it looked huge too; that you could walk for days, if not weeks, and never reach the other side. Down there, ground level, you realised it was all just an optical illusion though. The streets were littered and messy, with unhappy people walking around struggling to forge out a comfortable life and the scale of the city suddenly disappeared too. The alleyways and buildings all seemed to get closer, and almost pen you in. You were not as free as you thought you might have been.

Oh, to throw herself against that glass window and fall through. To land in a crumpled heap on the concrete below; her innards splattered across the sidewalk, adding to the city's grime.

Her mind skipped back to a report she'd read the previous week. A woman, not willing to go through with the pregnancy, killed herself to save the government going after her. They refused her a proper burial and threatened her family; if any of them so much as mourned her for a minute, they'd be punished with up to ten years in prison.

Whichever way she looked; she was trapped. At least for the next few months anyway. After that, all being well, she'd survive the pregnancy and could live out whatever life their new arrangement would afford them. If she survived.

As she slowly turned her mind back to the pile of paperwork at hand, a woman she recognised from the next floor up approached her desk and said, 'Tom just told me the news! Congratulations! I'm thrilled for you.'

And, like that, the bad thoughts were gone, and the forced smile was back in place.

'Thank you,' Cate said.

13

The end of the day had come, and Cate couldn't be happier. Well, with *that* aspect of her life at least. At home she could definitely be happier and that involved with being "not pregnant" but, there you go. She logged the computer off and stood up. Five months in and she was definitely feeling the ache in her back now. She stretched it out as best as she could and, to her relief, it gave a satisfying "click". A thought in her head: *Something else that would make me happier right now? A massage when I get home.* She laughed at the thought. Chances of that? If anything, it will be the other way round. He'll be bitching about his feet aching, after running around all day. He'll probably be the one asking for a massage. And, when she questions *what about her*? He'll have *that* answer ready; the one he's given her time and time before... *At least you get to sit down at work*. She shook her head as the conversation played through her head on repeat and, she started to gather her belongings together. She stopped when she realised everyone else had also stopped... They'd stopped their chatter, they'd stopped moving around, they'd stopped the last bits of work they were trying to get done before going home... They'd all just stopped.

Confused, Cate looked in the same direction everyone else seemed to be looking in. Four police officers were walking down the aisle between desks. Her boss was walking with them and, no sooner had Cate noticed them, he pointed her out to the officers.

Cate frowned and her heart skipped a beat as the men approached.

'Mrs. Hart?'

'Yes.'

'We're going to need you to come with us.'

'May I ask what this is about?'

She tried to put a brave face on and smiled at the officers in the hope of appearing "normal" and that she had nothing to fear from them. Her eyes betrayed her and were filled with fear. Everyone in the room was now watching her, unable to remove their eyes as though witnessing a car crash happen right before them. From the looks of some of their faces, she couldn't help but think that the only thing they were missing was a tub of popcorn.

'We've had reports.'

'About what?'

Cate was genuinely confused. As far as she was concerned, she'd been playing the role of "happy future-mother" quite well. To her knowledge, the only slip-up was with the shake during her last break. Surely that wasn't enough to get her reported though? She glanced in the direction of the colleague she'd been on break with. Even she looked confused as to why the police were there so - she wasn't the reason for their visit. Had it been her, and the shake incident, then she'd have no doubt had a smug look on her face as, it meant she'd be up for the reward they offered.

'That this is an unwanted pregnancy.'

All around her, people looked shocked. Cate mirrored their expressions so as to match.

'What?! That's rubbish!'

'Please, you're going to have to come with us.'

Two of the officers stepped forward. They each grabbed one of her arms and - despite her protests that she *wanted* her child, they marched her from the room and towards the elevators. Once they left, the room slowly returned to its normal hive of activity.

14

'Can someone please explain to me what is going on? I'm pretty sure everyone in the whole building knows I am pregnant now. They've all come and congratulated me, some even bought gifts. Not once have I complained about being pregnant or said that I didn't want it! I mean, what was I supposed to do? Announce it to the whole building? You're aware I don't know most of the people in there, right? I told a few people when we found out and now it's harder to hide... Now everyone knows... Again, not once have I said I don't want to have it! So, I ask again, what is this about because it sure as hell isn't about me not wanting the baby…'

Cate was sitting in the back of the police car. Two officers sat up front. Behind them, another car followed. She couldn't help but laugh when she saw it had taken two cars and four men to come and "collect" a pregnant woman. What were they expecting her to do exactly? Although, such a thought soon disappeared the moment she sat in the back of the car, and they slammed the doors shut. After that moment, panic set in deeper, eliminating all other thoughts.

One of the officers turned around and said, 'Lady, stop. Save yourself the embarrassment.'

'Embarrassment? The only ones who should be embarrassed as you! I've done nothing wrong and…,'

'Your husband came to the station and told us.'

Cate's heart skipped a beat. Her face dropped and - a moment later - she felt in flush. Her stomach swirled.

'Can you pull over? I think I'm going to be sick.'

The officer reached back and pulled a vomit bag from the back-pocket of the driver's chair. Without a word, he handed it to Cate and then turned to face forward once more.

Cate just sat there. Her mind raced with questions she didn't know she'd ever get the answers for. Why would he have gone to the police? Did he actually go, or was it part of their plan to get a confession from her?

The officer laughed. 'Seems your husband was struggling with the extra workload this brought about. Found it easier to come by the station and point out that neither of you wanted it.'

Still unsure, Cate said, 'I don't believe you.'

The officer turned in his seat again. 'Oh?'

'My husband and I are happy to welcome…'

'… A brother or sister for Hunter?'

Her heart skipped a beat at the mention of her son's name. But then, of course they could have found his name out without talking to Jack. Surely her son's name would have come up the moment they put her details into their system. It's not like his birth was a secret, or that he wasn't registered.

She continued her sentence, 'Yes. My husband and I are happy to welcome a brother or sister for Hunter.'

'Do you tell yourself that daily in the hope you're going to believe it one day?'

Silence.

The officer said, 'Or do you worry about surviving the pregnancy? Hunter nearly killed you when he came out of you... You don't stress that another baby *will* kill you? Meanwhile Jack stresses that you can't afford another baby?' The officer continued, 'Like I said, we know you don't want it so - why not stop lying to us and just be honest for once?'

Cate said nothing.

The officer shrugged and turned to face forward once again. For a while, they drove in silence. The other squad car still following behind.

Eventually Cate said, 'Do you know about my uncle? No, of course you don't.' She explained, 'He was involved in an accident. The doctors said he was brain-dead and that they were going to turn the equipment off, effectively letting him die. We didn't want them to touch it and, for a while they left it on. Eventually the courts stepped in and said the machines needed to be turned off and - as he was braindead - it wasn't violating any rights, or classed as murder... When you get pregnant, a foetus doesn't have consciousness until the cerebral cortex is formed, which happens in the second trimester... So, my question is, if before then - the foetus is technically brain-dead, how come it has more rights to live than someone who is pronounced brain-dead? Surely brain-dead is brain-dead? If you deal with it before the second trimester then, the foetus was never "living" so...'

'Because your uncle was a vegetable. No turning back for him. Done. The foetus has the potential of living so while it might not be living in that particular moment, as you put it... It *will* be living soon enough and it's not your right to say it can't have that life.'

There was no point in arguing with them. She knew that. Even so, if she was going to be in trouble for this then she may as well make it worthwhile.

'Do you two have partners?'

'Yes, thank you.'

'Do you have intercourse?'

'Of course.'

'Do you want children?'

They didn't answer.

'Okay well, if you don't... Did you get a vasectomy to try and ensure your partner doesn't get pregnant?' When they didn't answer she laughed. 'Or perhaps you two are partners to each other in more than one way?'

Without looking back, the officer said, 'You watch your fucking mouth, slut.'

Cate said nothing. The moment you're told to "shut your fucking mouth" is the moment all doors for discussion are closed. Even when you're in the right, the other party will never hear your words once you reach that point. And why? Because they know there could actually be a point to what you're saying. *Shut your fucking mouth*, what all people say when they have no further arguments to their side of the discussion.

15

TODAY

Delivery day.

With the birth imminent, Cate's medication had been cut back so that she could "push" when instructed to do so. She hadn't been removed from the wall although - with contractions taking place - the cups had been removed from between her legs. As another contraction tore through her, she screamed out in pain whilst a set of doctors carefully monitored her vitals.

Once in the room, the women didn't leave until after they'd given birth. Only once the baby was delivered safely were they removed from the wall and put onto a trolley before being wheeled back out by Claude, or one of his colleagues.

Today was Claude's first time in transporting a patient after the birthing process. Whilst a colleague took the baby to the nursery, he would take Cate through to recovery; a temporary room before being moved on again.

Being new, he didn't know much more about the process. The facility seemed to work on a need-to-know basis and all he needed to know was that patient A needed to be moved to this room, or that room... Occasionally he learned a little more, by watching or from gossiping colleagues but - other than that - he remained in the dark.

'Shouldn't we give her something for the pain?' Claude asked from the back of the room as he watched on, disturbed at how much she was screaming out.

The doctor laughed. 'Why think of her when she can't think of others? We don't waste what we don't have on those who don't deserve it.' He paused a moment and then turned to take a proper look at Claude. Unlike Claude, this wasn't the doctor's first day. He'd seen many births and heard many women screaming through the pain. That being said, he couldn't recall ever feeling pity for them. Not the women in this facility at least. He suggested, 'Perhaps you might want to wait outside if it is too much for you?'

Claude hesitated a moment, unsure whether it would make him look bad if he chose to step out. Then he thought, *fuck it*.

He was there to be transport for the patient, not to witness her give birth. Over the screaming, he explained, 'It's just my partner is pregnant... Our first one... I've not seen all this before, and I think... I think I'll step out so as not to live the next few months in a high state of anxiety, knowing she'll have to go through this.'

The doctor snorted and turned away, his attention back on Cate. Claude didn't wait for him to say anything else. Instead, leaving the trolley behind, he stepped from the room and out into the corridor, thankful for the room's heavy duty sound-proofing.

16

As he stood and impatiently waited outside
Room 101, Claude couldn't help but think
about Lauren and wonder how she was
going to cope with childbirth. More to the
point, he wondered if she'd be given any
pain relief to help ease the already difficult
process. He hoped so. Given what the
doctor said about wasting meds on those
who didn't deserve it, Claude also took that
as meaning pain relief *would* be available to
women who chose to have their baby,
without being forced. Claude couldn't help
but feel how fucked up this was. The

women were here, they were having their children… Surely that was all that mattered now? Why feel the need to punish them further by denying basic pain relief in what was undoubtedly one of the most traumatic experiences they could face? It was all just bullshit but then, part of him wondered why he wasn't really as surprised as he should have been? It was just another "fucked-up thing" to be added to an already long fucking list of reasons why the world was in the toilet. He sighed. No matter how much he tried to push these thoughts from his head, they always came circling back around but then, why wouldn't they? Nothing was improving. If anything, the world was getting worse, people were getting nastier and instead of the frustrated people turning to those who could do something about making positive changes, they simply turned on each other instead. For as long as the world was going to be as poisonous as this, Claude knew her negative thoughts would continue to plague him.

'You looking for a job?'

The voice startled Claude out from his head-space. A man in maintenance uniform was heading towards him with a metal case of tools in hand.

'No,' Claude said. 'Just waiting for a birth. Got to take the patient to the recovery room after she's done.'

The stranger laughed. 'Recovery room.'

Claude didn't understand what was so funny about that and frowned.

'Guess you're new here.'

'Well…Kind of,' Claude said.

The man laughed again. 'Not had time to go further down the rabbit hole then, hey.'

'What's that supposed to mean?'

'Just this place, man. Just this place. Once you think you've seen it all... There's always something around the corner that'll knock you for six.' He continued, 'Still, they brought it upon themselves.'

'Who did?'

Instead of answering the question, the man continued on down the corridor muttering to himself, 'Although I never understood why they called it the recovery room. Should have just saved money and had a trapdoor in the floor... Like Sweeney Todd...'

Sweeney Todd, the demon barber of Fleet Street, was a fictional tale about a barber who - seeking revenge - turned to killing his enemies whilst they sat in his barber's chair. A quick slit of their throat and, he pulled a level which opened a trapdoor down which he could tip their lifeless bodies. Claude understood the reference but not why Room 101 would benefit from such a set-up. As far as he was concerned, the women were taken down to the recovery room and - once "better" - released back home with their newborn baby and guidance on how to best cope now they had a new child in their life. There was no reason to doubt this was true. He went to call out but, the stranger - tools in hand and now whistling to himself - disappeared around the corner.

Claude was alone and confused.

17

Claude didn't know how long he had been sat out in the corridor; his back up against the wall - both metaphorically and literally. The automatic doors opened and the doctor stepped out. From behind him, one of Claude's porter colleagues wheeled the newborn out of the room and down the corridor.

'She's ready for you.'

Claude got up from the room and brushed himself down. 'Mother and baby are okay?'

'Pleased to report that the baby is healthy!' the doctor said with a smile, whilst ignoring the question about the mother. Claude didn't pick him up on this. What was the point? Like most other people working here, the doctor had made it pretty clear that he didn't rate the women as equals. To them, and a scary amount of people outside too, the women who wanted to abort were nothing more than second-rate citizens at best. Whilst Claude wanted to scream and shout at how fucked all of this was, he knew it would only serve to land him in the shit. His voice alone couldn't fix anything. As such, he walked into the room where the workers were strapping Cate to the waiting trolley.

They always strapped the exhausted women to the trolley after an incident soon after the facility opened which saw one particular woman make a hell of a mess. The poor bitch took the opportunity to try and run. She jumped up from the trolley and attempted to run down the corridor, only for her weak legs to buckle beneath her. So much after-birth splattered down on the white floors; a disgusting mess which someone had to come along and mop up. Since then: The women were strapped down at all times.

Another rule was that workers - the porters especially - were not to engage in conversation; not that many of the women were capable of talking, having been medicated and silent for so many months. Most just laid there and quietly wept through the day's trauma as they were wheeled away.

Despite the rule being in place, the moment Claude was out of the room and away from the other staff members, he asked, 'Are you okay?'

For whatever reason, she didn't answer.

Claude knew she had no reason to believe him but still reassured her as best he could, 'Everything is going to be okay now.' Even if she *did* believe him, even he didn't buy what he was trying to sell. Not with all the images of the Demon Barber planted in his head. Now, although they were heading to the recovery room, he had images of some maniac waiting there to slit her throat wide open. As it turned out, he wasn't far wrong although - a slit throat would have been kinder.

18

Claude's first time in the recovery room and it was as he expected. The same white decor as the rest of the facility. A long line of beds, either side of the long room - most occupied with women and most of those barely conscious. Just as they'd been wired up to various machines in Room 101, so too were they tangled with various tubes and cables in here too. Tubes to collect waste and tubes to give sustenance; the latter being about offering them the nutrients they needed now.

The only thing which took Claude by surprise was how quiet the room was. He expected women to be sitting up in their beds, chatting with one another - all grateful that their ordeal in the facility was coming to an end yet even the barely conscious ones showed no interest in talking, or being spoken to.

With a job to do, Claude transported Cate over to one of the spare beds. The room's workers came over and helped transport the exhausted woman from trolley to bed. Once done, Claude took a step back as they started plugging her in to the various apparatus. He left them to it and pushed his empty trolley back towards the exit point where the guard was waiting to sign the docket on Claude's file; proof that his "delivery" had been made.

'Papers?' the guard asked as Claude approached.

Claude handed the whole file over and watched as the guard flipped to the relevant page. While he waited, he said, 'Got to say, wasn't quite sure what to expect in here.'

'No?'

'Some maintenance guy... Said he didn't understand why they didn't just use trapdoors from Room 101.'

'Trapdoors?'

'You know, to get rid of the women after they've given birth.' Claude laughed. 'I was expecting some guy with a cut-throat razor in here.'

The guard signed the paperwork and closed the file. He handed it back to Claude who took it. 'Well,' the guard said, 'they weren't far wrong, were they? But, hey, got to spend the tax-payer's money some way, huh?'

Claude frowned. 'What are you talking about? This looks okay to me...' He glanced around the room, unsure as to whether he'd missed anything.

The guard laughed. 'Sure. It might *look* okay but...' He frowned. 'You really don't know what happens?'

Claude shrugged. 'I'm just the porter...'

The guard couldn't seem to understand how someone could wheel people around and not really know where they were taking them, or why, so he asked, 'You want to know what happens?'

Claude hesitated, unsure if he really wanted to hear the answer. Given the way the guard was being now, and what the maintenance man had said - *did* he really want to know? "They" say ignorance is bliss after all and yet, despite knowing this, he still answered, 'I guess.'

19

Claude hadn't touched a mouthful of his Chinese take-away; a rare treat they enjoyed once a month when both he and Lauren were feeling particularly lazy, not that she could enjoy it without accompanying it with her "pregnancy shake".

It was becoming a regular thing now; them sitting to dinner and him barely touching any of it. Watching him, anyone would think he had a sudden fear of food with how little he ate.

Just like other times, Lauren would watch for a moment and then she would ask if he was okay. He would say he was tired. Eventually he'd confess to not being hungry and cross his knife and fork over one another to signal that he'd finished. Although today he'd just be putting down his chopsticks. Lauren didn't say anything but, she was finding the whole dance tiresome.

'Tired?' she asked when she could stand the silence no more.

Claude nodded.

'Another long day?'

'It's all I seem to have,' he said.

With the exception of pushing Cate to the recovery room, Claude hadn't had much else to do today. A mercifully quiet day in the office, so to speak. Probably just as well given what the guard had told him about the recovery room and why the women were there. With that going around in his head,

Claude couldn't think of anything else. Unlike other facts about life which he didn't agree with, he also couldn't swallow it down and pretend it didn't exist either. It was lodged right at the front of his brain and nothing he could do, or think about, was seemingly able to shift it.

After another lengthy pause, Lauren said, 'You know, if the job isn't right for you…'

'It's fine.'

Lauren finished her sentence regardless, 'You don't have to do it. You can always give your notice and find something else.'

Claude smiled at her. If only it were that easy. The truth was - unemployment was at an all-time high. What few jobs there were, people were literally fighting over. In the news just the other week, someone didn't get a job they went for so, they went back to the office with a hand grenade. Not only did they kill themselves, but they also took six other people with them. More were injured. Competition out there was both fierce and violent.

Lauren knew Claude was stressing about the lack of other opportunities because, she'd seen how frantic he was getting before he found the current job. She said, 'We can cut back. While you look for something else, I mean... Cut back, get benefits... It might be hard but, we'll make it work just as we always have.'

'We're not claiming benefits.'

'Well then you can keep applying for other jobs while doing this one, can't you?'

Claude shrugged. He *could* apply for other jobs whilst working at the facility, that much was true. But what was also true was that, he didn't want another job. He didn't want *any* job. With all he was feeling inside, he'd simply had enough of everything. He knew he couldn't keep living with these feelings. He knew he had to either swallow it down and pick himself back up, or he had to talk to Lauren and let her try and help him through it. The problem with *that* was that she had enough on her plate and, especially whilst she was pregnant, he didn't want to add to her stress.

Stress?

His mind floated back to that poor woman screaming blue murder as she gave birth. Claude glanced up to Lauren and wondered if she knew the possible level of pain she was going to have to endure when the time came to give birth.

Confused with his expression, Lauren asked, 'What?'

Claude didn't want to talk about it for fear of scaring her. Instead, he smiled and said, 'I think I'm done.' He set his chopsticks to the side of the untouched plate.

'Did you want to put a film on, or something?'

'You know, I might just go to bed.'

'Long day?'

He nodded. 'Long day.'

20

BEFORE

11pm.

Jack stepped in the quiet house.

Their son, Hunter, was staying with Cate's sister. Jack had taken him round there earlier in the day, before heading to the police station. He didn't explain why, other than to say it was an emergency and he needed to take care of something. Had Cate's sister known what Jack had been planning, she might have tried to talk him down.

After confessing that they didn't want another baby, the police had issued Jack with a hefty fine. It could have been double what they actually set it to, and it still would have been cheaper than the cost of raising another child though.

As for Cate, the police had kept her in. When Jack asked after her, they told him that - under the circumstances - she wouldn't be going home any time soon. Instead, she would be transported to a government run facility where they could keep an eye on how her pregnancy progressed. When he asked whether he could see her, they said no.

Jack didn't know what he had been thinking when he went to the police. He hadn't thought through the bigger picture. He just knew he couldn't cope with the extra workload and pressure of having a baby. That, topped with the stress of whether the birth would kill his wife... His mental health simply cracked and, next thing he knew, he was standing in front of a pissed-looking detective.

As Jack stood there now, in the quiet of the house, he had a deep regret for how the day had played out and yet, he wouldn't have turned the clock back, even if he could have. What happened... What he did... It was for the best and, in time, he was sure his family and friends would agree with him... Except... He didn't think that at all. He knew that his own selfish actions hadn't just cost him his marriage but, they'd also go on to cost him his family and friends too. Then there was work. Would people be willing to work with him once they knew he reported his own wife to the authorities? Whilst it was the law to do so, it was rare that someone's own partner would step up and make the report themselves. Usually, they would plead ignorance and allow themselves to be arrested too. Again, the men would be fined and…

The thought went through Jack's mind that, he could always say someone else had made the report. But then, would the truth really stay buried? Everything tended to come out in the wash, and this would be no different. Sure, he could explain he was scared to say anything so made the lie up but then… He'd be a rat and a liar. No one wants that kind of person in their life.

Jack took his coat off and went to hang it on the peg by the front door. He missed and the clothing dropped to an untidy heap on the floor. He didn't pick it up. Instead, he made his way up the stairs and to the room he had once shared with his wife. In a trance-like state, he made his way across the carpeted floor, over to the cupboard in the far corner. He opened the door, reached in and pulled out a small metal box which he then took back to the edge of his bed, where he sat.

For a moment, he sat there. A little voice in his head said he should have done this first, instead of going to the police. He didn't have an answer for the voice, but then he didn't need to give it one. He knew it was right and - he flipped the lid of the box open and revealed the black handgun within.

This is the only way you might ever be forgiven.

If he did this, everything was sorted. His friends and family would still be angry with him, but they'd understand at least. They'd see that he felt trapped and pushed into a corner with no way out. They'd see the guilt he felt and how broken he was.

Jack picked the gun up and pressed it to his temple.

He closed his eyes.

Across the street, the neighbours woke to the sound of the gun shot. Unsure what was happening the man of the house ran for his own gun, just in case someone was going on the attack out there. If they dared come to *his* house, they'd be sorry. Gun in hand he told his wife to call for the police, unaware that - across the road - Jack's muddled brains dribbled down the wall.

21

TODAY

11pm.

Lauren woke with a start. Groggy from being yanked from a deep sleep, she looked over at the bedside clock and was shocked to see she'd only been asleep for an hour. It felt like much longer to her confused brain. Claude moved from the end of the bed again and, she twisted to see what he was doing.

'You scared me,' she said.

'Sorry.'

His voice was emotionless. She peered at him through the darkness to see if his face was too. If it was, she couldn't make it out.

'What are you doing?'

'Just sitting.'

'I thought you were tired?'

'Can't sleep.'

Every sentence came back in the same, flat tone. She knew it was her man sitting at the edge of the bed but, it still felt like it was a stranger sitting there.

Unsure what else to say, or do, she said, 'Come back to bed.'

He moved through the darkness and settled himself back down on the other side of the mattress on his back. She moved closer and cuddled in.

'I wish you would talk to me,' she said.

'I can't.'

'You can. I'm here. Whatever is on your mind, we can talk about it, and we can make it right. That's what couples do, right?'

He took a deep breath in and, still cold and emotionless, he confessed, 'I don't want the baby.'

Lauren didn't know what to say. At first she wasn't sure as to whether it was even some kind of weird joke that she just didn't understand. Before she could ask, he continued.

'The world is in a dark place. Has been for years. It seems every year we take a step backwards. The world is over-populated, resources running low, cost of living at an all-time high with more and more people losing their homes and such... The laws are getting stricter and everything just feels as though it is closing in. I'm suffocating and... We're about to bring someone else into the world to suffer through this too. It's not right. No… It's not *fair*. And people wonder why so many teenagers have emotional breakdowns and wish that they'd never been born? The world needs to be fixed. Rules and regulations need to be changed. Cost of living needs to come down and, everything just made easier. Tax the rich, not the poor. Let the billionaires pick up some tabs instead of forcing us to while they run about paying practically nothing to the government… Make it fair for us, the normal people and *then*… Knowing in mind that's all just the tip of the iceberg… Then it might be fair to bring a child into all this but until then, I can't do it…'

Lauren just laid there as he ranted. It was all well and good him saying this but, she wanted the baby. She saw the world through rose-coloured spectacles and, yes, it might have been a shit place but, there was hope that things would always get better. A foolish belief that the government was working for the people, not against them. Anyway, even if she disagreed with him, it wouldn't have done any good. She was pregnant. It was too late and there was no way she was going to go through this just to hand the baby over at the end of it all. *Sorry, we don't want this, please put it in the workhouse until someone decides to give it the love we couldn't.*

'The place I work... It really isn't what you think it is... What I've been pretending it is... It's Hell and... The government is running it like it's all perfectly normal and acceptable and... It makes you wonder - with how wrong this all is and how easy they seem to find it, and people to work there... What other facilities are they running behind fake brochures and false promises that everything is going to be okay?'

'What do you mean? What does happen there?'

Claude rolled onto his side and faced Lauren. Only now did he finally have tears in his eyes; tears which glistened in the narrow crack of moonlight which landed perfectly on his side of the bed.

'I'm sorry,' he said.

'What are you...'

Lauren froze as she felt the cold barrel press against her hefty stomach.

Claude told her, 'I love you. And, I would have loved the baby too... But this world isn't good enough for any of us...'

Before Lauren had a chance to respond, he squeezed the trigger of his Magnum and put a bullet straight through both mother and unborn child. In order to stop Lauren's suffering as quickly as possible, he put the remaining bullets into her. Then, only when she was still, did he finally weep.

It's for the best.

22

A new day and the same mood and ill-feeling to the world which had turned him into this; a monster splattered with his wife's dried blood.

Lauren's body laid cold in the bed. A sign of the times that no police had been called to investigate the noises. No doubt anyone who may have heard the shots simply ignored them because, it wasn't their problem, or they forced their brain to believe it to be something else. *Gee, that car sure is backfiring a lot*. Anything which would stop them from being disturbed or involved. Turning a blind eye never helps in the grand scheme of things though, does it? Instead of dealing with a problem, they just bury their heads in the sand and either hope it fixes itself or, they act all confused and shocked when the problem becomes worse. That was Claude's belief at least and, fresh from the shower, he'd be proving his own point today: *Everything can always get worse.*

As he stood in front of the mirror, looking at the unrecognisable shell staring back, he couldn't help but think today could have easily been avoided had someone just reported the shots during the night. In a way though, he was glad they hadn't. He needed today to happen. It was the only way he could truly express how he felt about his country… The country he once loved. The country he wished he could love once more.

Claude looked beyond his reflection to the bed behind him. His eyes didn't focus on Lauren. Instead, they fell upon his gun collection; handguns, rifles... All laid out, clips and magazines full and ready to go. His prized collection, including one which Lauren purchased for him as a "congratulations" for getting the job at the facility. He smiled to himself. That was the very same gun he was going to use to pop the head off the racist son of a bitch working in the incinerator room. For anyone else he ran into down there, he didn't give a shit what gun he used on them... But that motherfucker in the incinerator room? Lauren would have been proud it was her gun which killed him. A voice whispered in the back of his mind, *would she though*? He shook it from his mind and then fetched a sports bag large enough to carry as many weapons as he could realistically lift and lug around.

None of this was exactly planned. Unable to sleep, Claude had got out of bed during the night with an entirely different plan. He was going to grab his Magnum and, without much more thought needed, he was going to take it through to the ensuite and re-paint the walls with the inside of his head. But, no sooner was the gun in hand, did his mind sway. A thought that, suicide did nothing other than to hurt those around him. Even when there is a reason where people take their lives, the reason is more than often ignored. Instead, people focus on the dead person being mentally unwell. *Oh well, they couldn't have been helped.* Or they spend wasted time wondering, *why didn't they talk to us*? The reasons are pushed under the carpet as those close to the deceased turn to blaming themselves. Sitting on the edge of the bed, staring at the gun in the middle of the night, Claude knew he didn't want to be one of *those* statistics and that, if he was to die, he wanted his demise to mean something. If that meant he had to become the villain of the piece then, he was fine with that.

That was when *this* plan had come to mind.

He'd head to work as he always did. He'd clock in. He'd drink his morning coffee, if only to give him a little energy boost to bolster up the adrenaline. Then, he'd start with the semi-automatic weapon, pulling it from his bag and stalking the corridors and various rooms - shooting all those who worked there, whilst hopefully being careful not to hit any of the imprisoned women. Only once the bodies started to pile up would he take pause for a moment, once the sirens were heard in the distance. A brief break long enough to call the media channels to tell them who he was, what he was doing and why he was doing it... To tell them what was *really* happening within the cold thick walls of the facility. A burning question in his mind: Would he still be a villain if he were to expose an evil far worse? People might be outraged by his actions but, millions would be enraged by the actions of the government bodies allowing this facility to operate as it was and - if they got together then hopefully they could stop it from continuing. Hopefully, people could start to claim back their rights and put things back to how they were before the overturning of *Roe V. Wade* put everything into a spiral.

Claude turned back to his reflection. *It was a good job no one reported the gunshots.*

23

10am.

The corridor walls were splattered in claret wherever Claude had met a colleague. He didn't care if they were one of the "good" people, doing this for the money only. Each person there had a choice as to whether they wanted to stay quiet and get the work done or make a stand as Claude had. They chose the payday over "right and wrong" which, in his eyes, made them as deserving as the people who set up the facility in the first place. The only difference was, Claude could get to these fuckers, unlike those who sat in their fancy offices in an entirely different part of the country. Still, with all being well, what Claude was doing here would still reach those office-dwelling motherfuckers, albeit in a less violent way.

'Please, I don't want any trouble...'

Claude smiled at the piece of shit who ran the incinerator room. The barrel of his gun, pointed at the man's face, was still billowing smoke from the last shot taken. The man didn't smile back. He was just standing there, with his hands raised in a defensive manner, as if that could stop a round from hitting him.

'You don't want me to shoot you?'

'Please... I have a family.'

'And that matters because?'

'Because they fucking need me, man!'

'And the people you throw in the incinerator… They don't have a family that needs them? They don't have people who would want to see them again, or who would miss them?'

'They're fucking ni….'

Claude pulled the trigger. He didn't need the sentence finished to understand how it was going to end and, in all honesty, he didn't want to hear it. A human being is a human being, no matter where they come from and - people who don't see that… *They* are the ones who do not deserve to be here, using up the earth's precious resources and taking an unfair share of oxygen.

Claude turned from the room and headed up to the recovery room. He was thinking about this room during the night and, in his head, had come to the conclusion that the people working this wing were the worst of the bunch. The way he saw it, the ones in the rooms like Room 101, they were employed to keep people alive and to get the baby delivered safely. The ones in the so-called recovery room? They all knew what happened to the women from that room, where they went once well enough to leave... Again, they could have stood up for what was right, they could have quit the job when they discovered the truth but - no - they *still* chose to stay there. At least the people in Room 101, and pretty much most of the other departments to be honest, wouldn't have known - what with the departments being fairly secretive as to what took place within them. It's funny, Claude never really understood why the departments were so secretive about their role and now, finally, he "got it".

He turned the corner. A man was standing there. The moment he saw Claude he scr.... Dropped to the floor with a smoking hole in the centre of his forehead and the inside of his skull peppered on the white wall behind. There was something quite artistic about how the gore looked, painted onto the blank white canvas. The really fucked up thing about this new world? Some art critic would probably pay millions for it, had they been able to. But then, would it be worth millions when there are so many examples of this piece dotted around the facility? And Claude wasn't done yet.

He dropped the empty gun and pulled another from the bag hanging from his aching shoulder. *I'll be needing ice in the morning,* he thought to himself as he continued his path of destruction.

24

When women went into the recovery room, they did so malnourished and weak. In the rooms prior to this one, they had been barely kept alive. The nutrients given, just enough to ensure they didn't pass away with *more* nutrients being pumped directly to the child within.

On paper, the recovery room was the place to be. Once inside, the women were pumped full of everything their body was lacking and more. They were brought back to the healthiest possible level and, it was done within the quickest amount of time too thanks to the various infusions. This wasn't for the patients' benefit. This was because they wanted them processed and for the bed to be ready for the next person who needed it.

And what were they to be processed for?

When the women were healthy, they were taken into a room off to the rear of the recovery room. Within the walls of this next room, there was a giant blender which spun continuously with its jagged, sharp teeth. The teeth themselves stained in red with bits of dried "meat" plastered to them in various spots.

It didn't matter that the women screamed because, like all other rooms within the facility, these four walls were also lined with the thickest of sound-proofing materials. *Scream all you want, there ain't nobody that's gonna hear ya.*

The women were pulled from their wheelchair by however many staff-members it took. Then, kicking and screaming, they were tossed into the machine's hungry jaws and chewed upon by its razored teeth. The pulp and juice left behind dribbled down through the narrow gap between spinning mechanisms and into a large filtration system. The larger chunks of pulp were kept for the older children and the goo and juice that went through the holes was kept for the hungry infants who'd not yet progressed to solids.

All of this was done because scientists had discovered a way to make a new weapon; an ultra-violent, sadistic creature which resembled a man yet barely acted as one. All they had to do was give a mixture of this "food" in with the normal food, starting the children from when they were first drinking milk although, at that age, it would be just a drop. Enough to give them a taste and to start preparing their body to be able to take more as they get older. No one knew why exactly but, by giving them this taste from birth, it altered the minds and twisted the brain into something more murderous and, always hungry for more. To speak in terms of fiction: A zombie of sorts, despite the fact that these creatures - in Claude's reality - were living, breathing beings as opposed to members of the undead, shuffling along.

None of the children were released from the facility's care. They were moved to another building and trained up from young. They didn't know any better. For them, this was what "life" was about. Then, when an overseas issue popped up in which America couldn't just drop bombs, the children were slowly starved from their supply of the mixture, instead eating "normal" food. The less you gave them of the mix, the more they craved it. The more they craved it and, the hungrier they got. Then, and only then, were they transported to the country in which the conflict was happening. They were dropped off with no food and told, this was their home now. Survival instincts would kick in soon after and they'd go on a violent, bloody rampage - killing and eating whoever they could reach before being put down themselves. The whole thing was bloody and barbaric and, today, the whole thing would be coming to an end.

Claude stood in the recovery room's doorway with a semi-automatic rifle in hands. With no sense of satisfaction or glee, he opened fire. Barely able to control the weapon, some bullets bit into the walls, some rained down on the bedridden patients there and others punched through the intended targets.

Claude didn't stop firing until the room was still and, even then he gave one extra spray of bullets just to be sure all were dead. *Don't feel bad for them, they had a choice as to whether they wanted to work there or not. Only a monster would be comfortable in such an environment.*

Claude lowered his gun. He took one hand off and reached for his phone. Now was a good a time as any to make the call to the media, to tell them what he was doing and why. Then, let them finish telling his story whilst he went to be with Lauren and his child. A simple plan but one which, he hoped, would be effective.

Fuck this place. Fuck this world.

25

Security led the armed police through the facility's winding corridors. All men running with their fingers close to the triggers.

Each new corridor showed more signs that they were on the right path with bodies, blood and bullet-holes; an "impressive" distance covered by one man in what had - in reality - been a short amount of time, and that was without even seeing the damage he'd done in the rooms leading off from the corridors.

Security had been keeping watch of Claude from the moment he first opened fire. None of them being trained to a comfortable enough level to tackle him themselves, they called for the authorities to come. Now, one man remained in the office talking his team through to where Claude was sitting, via their headsets.

Claude was sitting on the end of Cate's bed. He had a tear rolling down his cheek but, it wasn't due to the bloody cover over Cate's body, or the hole in her motionless chest. It was for the phone-call he'd just had.

Claude had expected the media to drive to the facility, desperate to cover the story as it unfolded. He'd presumed they would have spread the word too - or that, at the very least, all channels kept a close eye on each other just in case one got a scoop the other had missed.

Claude expected a number of news-vans to screech into the parking lot, the presenters to jump out with their team and immediately go "live" - even cutting into shows already playing in the various stations. *Sorry to interrupt your program but we have breaking news just in...* He'd explained what he was doing there but, before he could get much further, they'd cut him off by saying that it wasn't a slow news day so, they didn't need *another* mass-shooting story. He tried to get the rest of the story out but, they disconnected the call.

A different tact then, he thought. *Call them back and report the facility first and then...*

The door to the recovery room swung open and the cops led the way in with their guns raised and pointed straight to Claude. Startled by the sudden intrusion, even though he'd been expecting it at any moment, Claude jumped up with phone in one hand, and a pistol in the other.

One officer yelled, 'Put the gun down, or we'll open fire!' It was a sentence which Claude couldn't help but to laugh at. 'Put the gun down!'

Claude didn't put the gun down though. Instead, he said, 'I have something in my hand which can kill you and yet, still… I've been given a choice of what to do.' He paused a moment, wondering if the officers get what he was referring to; the fact that they were in a facility which stripped all choice from the "patients" there, despite these "patients" posing no threat to anyone else. Yet here he was, a direct threat to them and, he was given a choice. He asked them,

'Do you not see how fucked up this world is?'

'Put the gun down, asshole!'

'More so,' Claude continued, 'when you realise that, had my skin been a different colour... This story would have already been ended...'

'Just put the fucking weapon down!'

Claude laughed. Then, he shook his head. 'No,' he said, 'I don't think I'll be doing that for you.' The moment he finished his sentence, he went to point the gun to the officers and... Before the barrel had barely moved an inch, he dropped to the floor with the Taser's barbs sticking in his chest...

It really is a fucked up world we live in.

Made in the USA
Columbia, SC
19 September 2023

23062017R00093